Cristina L. Hardrich resides near Annapolis, Maryland. She is passionate about boating, the beach, reading, writing, crafting, decorating, going to the movies, family time, animals, and meeting with friends. Ms. Hardrich works as a full-time nurse at a busy middle school. In addition, she works several shifts per month at an urgent care facility. She graduated from college with a bachelor's degree in psychology, education, and years later, earned a degree in nursing. She has four children, one grandson, one dog, and two cats. She always had a passion for writing and is thrilled to publish *Do Not Think About Pink Elephants*.

Do Not Think About Pink Elephants

Cristina L. Hardrich

AUSTIN MACAULEY PUBLISHERS™

LONDON • CAMBRIDGE • NEW YORK • SHARJAH

Ordering Information:
Quantity sales: special discounts are available on quantity purchases by corporations, associations, and others. For details, contact the publisher at the address below.

Publisher's Cataloging-in-Publication data
Hardrich, Cristina L.
Do Not Think About Pink Elephants

ISBN 9781645751694 (Paperback)
ISBN 9781645751687 (Hardback)
ISBN 9781645751700 (ePub e-book)

Library of Congress Control Number: 2020902248

www.austinmacauley.com/us
First Published (2020)
Austin Macauley Publishers LLC
40 Wall Street, 28th Floor
New York, NY 10005
USA
mail-usa@austinmacauley.com
+1 (646) 5125767

Dedicated to my father,
Douglas Robert Hardrich.

Sometimes, I have a bad day.
Sometimes, I am in a bad mood.
Daddy does not like seeing me
in a bad mood.
Daddy has a way of making me laugh.
Even when I feel like I cannot smile.
But not today.

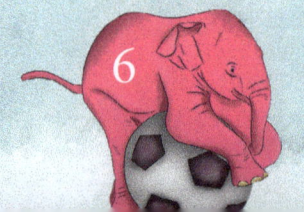

"Daddy," I said, "I am in no mood to smile or laugh, so please leave me alone." "Ok Lisa," he said. But his eyes twinkled. I knew what he was thinking. "No daddy," I said. "Don't even try it!" Your tricks will not work today, I thought. I am far too angry today to smile.

Today, my teacher gave me a bad grade.
She said my handwriting was messy.
It looked neat to me!
That was just the beginning.
At recess, I wanted to play "birdies"
with Ann.
But she was playing on the swings
with Sandy.
Ann was my best friend.
This day just kept getting worse.

At lunch, my juice spilled on Sophie's lap.
She thought I did it on purpose.
Sophie would not talk to me.
Then, on the bus ride home, Tommy
called me ugly.
"You're ugly!" I shouted back at Tommy.
He just laughed.
This made me very angry.

No, there was nothing to smile
about today.
I knew no matter how much I protested,
Daddy would still try to make me smile.
I was in a bad mood. I was mad.
"Daddy," I said, "nothing you can say or
do will make me happy."
"I don't know about that Lisa," he said
with a smirk.
"Whatever you do," he started. "Do NOT
think about pink elephants."
"Really Lisa, and whatever you do,
do not smile."
I won't, I thought. I stood with
my arms crossed.

"Ok Lisa," he kept going.
"Just do not smile, do not laugh, and whatever you do, do NOT think about a purple hippopotamus with hiccups."
He giggled out loud.

Sometimes, just the look on daddy's face would make me laugh.
Not today.
No way can he make me smile today and I definitely was not going to laugh!
But, Daddy continued.
"Lisa, I really want you to stay mad," he said. "So, whatever you do, do NOT think about a zebra with yellow,
blue and green stripes."

Oh, daddy was on a roll.
He really thought he was funny...
So funny, in fact, he had the tendency to
laugh at his own jokes.
Sometimes, I could not help it.
Sometimes, I had to laugh.
His silliness could be contagious.

I started to feel the corner of my lips curving up. I was forming a smile.
No! He would not win.
I was really, really, really mad!
I was crossing my arms and had a frown on my face.
I looked down at the ground because I could not look Daddy in the eye.
He knew how to make me smile and I wasn't going to let him!
Out of nowhere, I could not remember what had made me so angry.
As I tried to remember, I heard him say, "Lisa, whatever you do, do not think about a blue monkey riding on a tall red giraffe."
"Do not smile Lisa," he said. "And for goodness sake, whatever you do, do NOT laugh!"

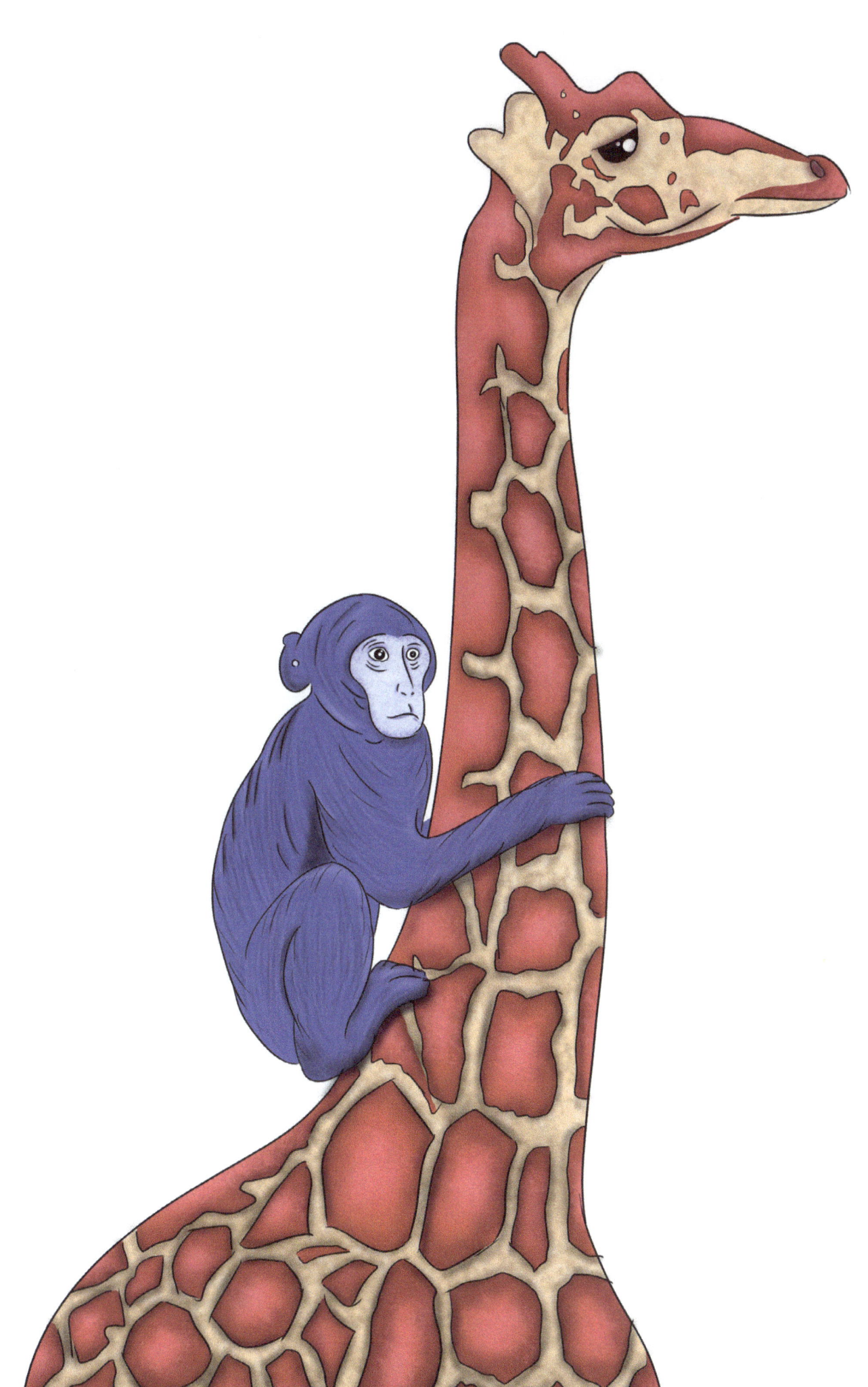

Now, Daddy had his arms crossed.
He was walking in circles around me.
I kept looking at the ground.
"Lisa," he said laughing, "Whatever you do, do NOT think about cross eyed rabbits playing leap frog in the park. Oh no! And whatever you do, DO NOT LAUGH."
He was so ridiculous, I thought.

He fell on the floor laughing.
He could barely catch his breath.
I do not know where it came from.
Out of the blue, a huge smile swept
over my face.

Whatever I did, I could not stop thinking
about silly zoo animals.
And I really could not stop myself
from laughing!
Daddy won.
His laughter alone could
make anyone smile.
I was now on the floor with him, laughing
harder and harder.
To my surprise, I wasn't mad anymore.
My super bad day did not
have to stay bad. Right?
By now, Mom had come down the stairs.
She stood there in silence and watched us
laugh and carry on.
She was smiling.
How can you not smile, while watching
two of your favorite people laughing and
having fun?

I thought I would play his
little game back.
I squealed, "Daddy, whatever you do, do
NOT stop laughing."
This made him laugh harder.
Oh boy, I thought.
This was going to be a long night.